BLEED FOR CUPID

A Word of Warning

Bleed for Cupid is a dark monster romance novella containing graphic scenes that may be triggering for some.

Trigger/Content Warnings: graphic sex, gore, violence, breathplay, bloodplay, bondage, dubious consent, drink spiking, discussions of parental death and murder.

Also note that this is a 21,000-word novella. If you're looking for something plot-heavy, this may not be the book for you. If you're looking for a quick and angsty read about our heroine becoming mates with a demonic Cupid, then read on...

1

CALLUM

"Do I have to force it down her throat?"

I ground my teeth, but the piece of shit sitting across from my desk didn't notice. He was too busy throwing back the two fingers of whiskey I'd poured him.

Swinging my attention to my own glass, I downed the last of the amber liquid, enjoying the burn. Liquor was a must during these meetings. Otherwise, I wouldn't be able to tolerate these rich fucks who always asked the same stupid questions about Cupid's line of love potions.

How do I make them take it?

Do they have to drink the full bottle?

Does it really alter fate, or is it just an aphrodisiac?

All questions that could be answered if they just read the back of the fucking bottle.

Normally, I wouldn't give our customers the time of day. Supernaturals looking for love solutions could walk into any number of our retail partners and purchase our products. If they had an issue, that was what the customer service line was for. As the CEO, I didn't deal with that shit.

But the man sitting across from me wasn't a regular

customer. This was a lion shifter who owned a chain of successful strip clubs, and was one of my original investors. If it weren't for him and his money, Cupid Inc. would have never been resurrected from the ruin my father left it in.

Now I had to smile, take his calls and pretend I didn't want to bash his skull in with my bare hands.

"You don't have to force it down her throat, Riggs. In fact, I recommend a more discreet method." I poured myself another finger of whiskey and, with my glass in hand, I rose from my chair and strode to one of my office windows.

I narrowed my eyes at the protesters cluttering the street below, a bitter taste forming on my tongue that had nothing to do with the alcohol.

Fucking human protesters.

It was funny how they hadn't given a shit about my company or what I was selling back when we were exclusively a brand for supernatural beings. But the moment they caught wind that we were developing love potions for humans, all hell broke loose.

"Yes, discretion," my guest rumbled. "You know you've sunk low when *I'm* almost too embarrassed to be seen here, Reaver."

My fingers flexed around the glass. I didn't like the fact that my reputation had fallen lower than this slime bag's, who was known for building his fortune off the backs of the poor women who worked for him.

I twisted around, teeth gnashing. "Then why *are* you here, Riggs?"

"Your father may have started this company, but he's gone. You are Cupid Inc. You rescued it from ruin. Even though you've gotten yourself into a PR nightmare with the humans, you're still a legend."

"A legend," I muttered bitterly as I turned my attention back to the window, glaring down at the protesters below.

My father had been the one to create the magic we bottled today. But I was the one to mass produce it and make it readily available to any scumbag supernatural. He'd been the legend.

I was a menace.

A monster.

"I'm here because I am in need of your services," Riggs continued. "I'm in love with a girl who used to work for me. Paying her for her companionship worked for a little while, but she grew bored. I want her to *crave* me. To worship me."

I took another sip from my glass. "You want to own her, body and soul."

"Fuck, yes," Riggs groaned, a bead of sweat sliding down his temple.

I turned away from the window, arching a brow. He really was crazy for this woman, whoever she was. He looked like he was on the edge of shifting at the mere thought of her. I understood the maddening desire affecting him, his feral need for the woman who held his senses captive.

"If the gods were less cruel, they would have made her my fated mate."

I wagged a finger at him. "I'm going to stop you there. Naturally fated mates aren't the work of a god, Riggs. I know because the gods aren't real."

He stared blankly at me. "But you're an angel."

Irritation flashed in my eyes, which he noticed, going by the way he shifted uncomfortably in his chair. "Yes. And Heaven is anarchy, Mr. Riggs. The phenomenon of the chemical reaction between supernatural beings known as fated mates is nothing but the primal urge to fuck and reproduce. Biology. Science.

Cupid Inc.'s products are just that: Fate in a bottle. All you have to do is make her drink it. If spiking her drink isn't working, then perhaps you should consider your previous solution of forcing it down her throat. Just be discreet about it. The last thing I need is more media attention. My profits are down as it is."

"I already did that."

My smile disintegrated. "That's impossible."

Riggs' brows bent into a scowl. "You saying I'm a liar?"

"I'm saying that I didn't spend a nauseating amount of money on product testing not to be certain that if so much as a drop hits your intended mate's tongue, she'd be licking the ground at your feet right about now."

"Seeing as that's not the case... what do you suggest?"

"I'm suggesting that she's a human."

"Well, yes."

I glared at him, then pinched the bridge of my nose. No matter who the customer was—a hillbilly werewolf looking to steal the affections of the local tavern's barmaid or a middle-aged, billionaire lion shifter with an obsession with a human stripper half his age—no one ever read the damn small print.

"It doesn't work on humans, Riggs."

"That's interesting since, last time we met, you told me you were pouring all my funding into engineering the human-compatible formula."

For some reason, the mention of Cupid's Arrow struck a nerve. Then again, every word out of Riggs' mouth pissed me off. "The Cupid's Arrow formula was in the trial stages. It needs humans for testing, but I called off the trial studies, at least until this PR nightmare cools down."

"Don't you have a human that works for you?" The shifter donned a skeevy smirk. "That pretty piece of ass you have for a secretary. What's her name? Robin?"

A wave of possessiveness suddenly surged through me,

and my fingers flexed so tight around my glass, it shattered. I swore, clenching my bloody fingers. "I appreciate your funding, Riggs, I do. But if you comment on my secretary's body ever again, I'll make you regret it."

More sweat poured down the shifter's temples, soaking the collar of his shirt. He laughed awkwardly. "I get it. Guess I'm not the only one with my sights set on a human female." He stood up, nudging the suitcase he'd brought in and left beside his chair. "You should find this to be enough to resume testing on Cupid's Arrow. Because it looks like I am not the only one with a personal stake in its success."

With that, Riggs turned heel and left my office.

Good fucking *riddance*.

I hated him for putting an idea in my head that I'd worked so hard to push away. He was right. I wanted my secretary, and had since the first day she'd started working for me. But I had no intention of claiming her for my mate.

Cupid Inc.'s love potions were evil. That was just a fact. They forced attraction for people who weren't interested in a particular partner, altering their brain chemistry to have the equivalent desire of a fated mate.

What I hadn't told Riggs was that Cupid's Arrow was already formulated. It needed a few more tests, then it was good to go.

But I wouldn't be releasing it to the market.

It was a step too far.

Humans were soft, delicate creatures. They weren't meant to be with supernaturals—especially hybrids like me. Robin had shown interest in me over the years, but she'd never seen my true form. If she had, she'd have seen me for the true monster I was.

And she'd be terrified.

So, while using Cupid's Arrow on her would ease her

fears and manipulate her heartstrings in my favor, I wouldn't do it.

If I were to mate her, I'd break her.

There was a light tapping on my office door, and then the sweetest, songbird-like voice called my name on the other side. "Mr. Reaver? Mr. Riggs said that you're bleeding. Can I come in?"

Fuck. Even her voice made me hard. I took a breath, steeling myself. "You may enter."

2

CALLUM

Robin had worked for me for just over three years. She'd come to the company shortly after I'd inherited it from my late father. I hadn't intended on hiring a human for my secretary, especially since every other Cupid employee was supernatural.

Cupid Inc. wasn't a place for humans. But then *she* had waltzed her perfect ass into my office for an interview. The glorious scent of the rose shampoo she still used to this day had flooded the air, and her green eyes had shot right through me like an arrow to my heart. And when she'd handed me her resume, her fingers had brushed mine.

I'd nearly lost it.

When supernaturals with two forms lost control, it was common to shift into their beast form without meaning to. By some miracle, I'd held it together through the interview.

I'd hired her. Not because I was obsessed, but because she was damn qualified. My infatuation for her had been a nuisance. If it weren't for her constant presence, I could walk around my building in my true form. It did put off the other supernaturals—it was probably all the eyes—but at least they wouldn't run screaming. And if they called me monster, I wouldn't spare two fucks.

It was different with her.

As a dark angel that ran a multibillion-dollar business with a dark reputation, there wasn't much that got to me. But the thought of her hating me? Of her seeing my true form for the first time and cringing? It made my black little heart ache.

So with her, I kept up the appearance of being civilized, normal. As if the mere thought of her didn't make my mind light up with twisted thoughts of her naked body and how it might look bent over my desk.

Maybe it was because I'd kept up the facade for years now, but when I was with Robin, I almost felt human. Like I wasn't an evil hybrid abomination that peddled my father's glorified date-rape drugs.

It was a nice little lie.

When Robin strode into my office, I snapped my mask in place; a pleasant little smile that felt all wrong on my face.

She was almost too gorgeous to look at. I wasn't sure how I'd managed to keep my sanity every day for the past three years. Her long, chestnut hair was in a bun high on her head today. Her form was curvy, with thick thighs wrapped in milky-white flesh that peeked out from her pencil skirt. Her middle was soft and slightly rounded, and her breasts were full—the perfect size to slip my cock between.

Shit. I was doing it again; imagining her naked body beneath mine, her flesh pink and swollen from my ministrations.

She was too beautiful for the likes of me, and certainly too fragile. Still, I allowed myself to indulge in the fantasy that she was mine to break from time to time.

"Little bird," I said in a cool greeting that wouldn't betray my dirty thoughts.

Hearing my nickname for her, her eyes flickered to the corner of the room where the floor-to-ceiling cage sat. My father had had the enclosure installed when he'd first bought the building, to keep his doves in. White feathers were a signature of Cupid Inc., and he'd thought the birds made for good pets.

When my father had passed, he'd left them to me, along with everything else in the building. And just like everything else in this godforsaken hellhole, they reminded me of him, so they hadn't gotten the attention they'd deserved. I supposed Robin hadn't liked seeing the poor things locked up. So her second week in, she'd opened the cage along with the windows and set them free.

I'd taken to calling her little bird ever since.

She paused for a second, biting that plump bottom lip in a way that had me groaning internally. Her gaze dropped to my hand. "You're hurt."

"I'll be fine."

She rolled her eyes at me, something no other employee of mine would dare to do in my presence. "Sir, you're dripping blood all over your shoes. Knowing you, you spent more on those shoes than what I make in a month."

I chuckled. "Not true."

I paid Robin a ludicrous amount, more than any of my other employees. That included my security, my chief scientists, my tech team, my sales representatives and my marketing team. Hell, she made more than some departments put together. "You *know* that's not true."

She gave me a small smile that made my heart twist and my cock twitch. She was so beautiful, especially when she smiled.

I pictured running my tongue over the seam of her mouth, tasting the flavor of her lips. I was so lost in the image, I didn't notice her going to the bar for a rag until she'd already returned and was bent over in front of me, wiping the mess at my feet.

"You don't need to do that. I can clean up after my own messes."

She tilted her head, peeking up at me through her thick lashes. "I don't mind, sir."

"Careful with the glass. I don't want my little bird to get hurt."

She ran her tongue over her lower lip, wetting her flesh. "A little pain doesn't bother me."

Christ. I was so fucking hard at the sight of her bent over in front of me. That damn pencil skirt and the way the fabric hugged her thighs and wide hips had my mouth watering.

She was too close to me, closer than I'd normally let her get. Her scent was overpowering, invading the defenses I put up against her.

This female. There was something about her that called to those monstrous urges buried deep within me.

Over the years, I'd become a master at maintaining control. She almost never wore skirts, though, and judging by the strength of her feminine scent, I'd say my sweet little bird wasn't wearing panties today.

I needed distance between us. I didn't trust myself not to join her on the floor and confirm my no-panties theory.

Striding to my desk, I collapsed in my chair and set to plucking the glass shards from my hand. I wasn't sure how much time had passed. I lost focus of my hand, slipping back into my thoughts. Today wasn't a good day as far as my concentration went.

My mind wandered to my father. Would he be proud of me? That I had kept his company and resurrected it from the ashes? Doubtful. He'd probably punish me over the fact that I'd yet to find the mole leaking company intel to the anti-super-natural organization responsible for terrorizing every store corner that sold my products and reaping this quarter's profits.

What would he do? Probably kill everyone on the payroll and start fresh, that would take care of the company's little confidentiality issue. For an angel, my father had been an evil fuck.

I'd thought about wiping the slate clean, but... I glanced back at Robin. Her mere presence made me a better man than my father.

Even though we could never be together, she made me want to be better.

I never would be.

But with her, the desire was there. It always was.

When she caught me staring at her, I forced my attention back to my desk and pretended to busy myself with my computer. In my periphery, I saw her rise to her feet and approach my desk.

"Robin, clear my schedule for the rest of the day. I have a meeting scheduled with the CFO today, but I can't deal with that now."

"I'll call Mr. Lyle and tell him you had something come up."

"Thank you—" My words latched in my throat when she grabbed the bottle of whiskey from my desk and sat herself down in my lap.

"Robin, what are you—"

"Shhh."

Her shushing sounds morphed into a soft whimper when my hand darted out, seizing her dainty wrist holding the bottle.

"Don't 'shhh' me. Don't *ever* 'shhh' me," I cautioned her in a dark, demonic voice that had her freezing in my lap.

There was a part of me that terrified her. It was written all over her blotted skin. Yet, she was a brave little thing. Her eyes lit up with that spark of defiance, and her heart beat a powerful tune, like a war drum.

She was scared, but today was a day where her curiosity overrode her fear.

If she only knew the kind of fire she was playing with.

"I'm sorry," she said in that honey-sweet voice. But she didn't climb out of my lap, and today, I didn't have the willpower to make her.

My cock throbbed painfully as she placed her plump thighs against my hips and settled her bare pussy against the crotch of my slacks.

No panties. I was certain now. I could feel the heat of her juicy center seep into the thin barrier of fabric between us.

She took the bottle of whiskey and poured it over my hand to sterilize the wound. It wasn't necessary since I couldn't get infections, but I didn't stop her. I was too lost in her touch.

As she worked to clean my wounds, my mind ran riot. I thought about what it would be like to lay her out on my desk and rip her clothes off.

I'd pictured her naked so many times. Would she be as supple as I imagined? Would her nipples be as pink and rosy as her lips when she suckled them every time she caught me looking at her?

Would her large tits fill my hands as well as I expected?

When I inevitably lost control and shifted into my true form, would she tremble in fear? She knew I was an angel, so she probably expected the eyes. What she didn't know was that I was a hybrid, and my mother had been a demon.

My demonic blood affected parts of me that would leave a substantial mark on any mate I took in the future.

I wasn't a gentle lover. My tastes in the bedroom were what you might expect from a half-incubus who watched his mother die at the hands of his father. Sex demons were wicked enough without piling on crippling childhood trauma.

Then there was my physical size. My cock would break her.

Still, I couldn't stop myself from imagining her little pink pussy stretching to take me.

A delicious whimper bled from her throat as she felt the way she was affecting me. She squirmed in my lap, batting her lashes at me. "You never let me get this close to you."

I tensed. "You know why."

"You don't scare me."

"You're lying."

She worried her bottom lip. "Fine. Maybe you do a little. But that's always because you're telling me you're dangerous, that you're not like the angels in human stories. But I don't care. I want to touch you. Please, sir."

Hearing her call me "sir" made my cock so hard, I was sure she could feel it now. She'd been calling me that for years. I was her boss, so the honorific wasn't anything inappropriate. At least, it hadn't been at the start. The word carried more power now, especially with the way she slowed down to taste it every time, her lashes fluttering and her body heating in the same way it might if I asked her to start calling me daddy.

"I might lose control and shift."

"I'm not scared," she said. It was practically a purr.

My gods. She was so sweet, so beautiful. And today, she was bolder than usual.

I wondered what the occasion was, but only for a moment. "If you're not scared, then kiss me."

Her plump lips parted on a soft gasp, surprised by my request. "Where would you like your kiss?"

Fucking hell. This female was going to be my ruin. I wasn't sure how to answer her question. I wanted her mouth in such unspeakable ways, I didn't trust myself to speak.

I didn't have to, though. She could see my answer entwined with the dark thoughts playing behind my eyes.

When she climbed out of my lap, I figured she'd lost her nerve. I watched her take a drink of my liquor before setting the bottle down on my desk, and then she lowered herself to her knees before my chair.

I followed her gaze to where it was affixed to the wet spot she'd left on the fly of my slacks. Ever so slowly, her hand reached for the zipper of my pants.

This time, I didn't stop her.

3

ROBiN

allum had been right. I was a liar. I was scared shitless. However, I wasn't afraid he'd hurt me.

At least, not in any way I wouldn't like.

What I was afraid of was finally crossing that line we'd been dancing for years. Not because he was supernatural—even if there were whispers of him being only half angel, half something *else*.

I was afraid of getting too close to him. Eventually, he'd find out what I'd done.

Maybe then, he'd actually hurt me. And probably not in the fun kind of way. At first I thought I was doing the right thing by joining the anti-supernatural organization terrorizing Cupid Inc. and all its customers. I wanted to bring the company crashing down to its foundation. And at one point, I'd wanted to take down its owner right along with it.

But then he died, and his son took over Cupid Inc. On paper, Callum Reaver was as evil as his father. I'd figured that out when I'd stumbled across the files for the Cupid's Arrow project.

That's when I'd reached out to the anti-sup group. They'd encouraged me to seduce Callum so he wouldn't catch on to the fact that I was the mole. Maybe that's what pushed me over the line today to finally touch him.

I'd be lying if I said I hadn't felt a pull toward him for years.

What had started out as innocent curiosity had morphed into something dangerous and lustful. The dark and beguiling chemistry between us had turned me into a total simp for my boss. Then, it had gotten complicated after I'd discovered the true depths of Callum's depravity.

Angels were supposed to be good.

Callum Reaver wasn't. Still, I wanted him anyway. It was his father's evil-ass corporation and fucked-up legacy that I wanted to burn to the ground. And I couldn't do that without hurting him. Once he discovered my betrayal, it would be the end of us before there had even been a beginning.

I couldn't shake the guilt that came with betraying him, which just pissed me off all over again. He was a horrible, greedy man. He didn't care about me, not really. At least, that's what the anti-sups kept telling me. If he cared about humans at all, he wouldn't have started developing a formula that would force them to be attracted to supernatural beings.

So here I was, on my knees before Callum and about to suck his dick because that's what was needed of me from my organization. It was my duty to throw him off the trail so I could keep my position as the group's inner ear. It had nothing to do with the fact that I had actually been in love with him for three years.

Maybe if I kept telling myself that, it would be true.

My hand shook as I pulled down the zipper to his Armani slacks. I felt his eyes burning into me. His hand covered mine, and I peered up to find him staring at me with an expression that had my heart twisting.

"You don't have to do this if you don't want to."

My eyes locked with his. There it was. Traces of the angel inside, staring at me through his cerulean orbs.

There had to be more to Callum than everyone said. Maybe he was just trying to uphold his father's legacy.

He was a good son.

A good boss.

And he was good to me.

"I want to." This time, I wasn't lying.

I pulled out his erection, trying to keep the surprise off my face.

Geez. He was huge. I didn't know much about his "true" form, but I knew it was larger than this one. It was hard to imagine a cock much bigger than the one in front of me. It was heavy in my hands, with silky smooth skin and a head that was already gleaming with pearly beads of pre-cum.

Callum arched his dark eyebrows at me.

Holy hell, was he gorgeous with his slicked-back hair that was as black as his heart. His perfect lips curved into a sinful smile that would look right at home on Satan himself. "My kiss?"

I leaned down, pressing my lips to his head. He shuddered, and an erotic groan fell from his lips when I painted a long lick up his shaft, stretching from his balls all the way to the slit of his tip.

"*Fuck*, Robin. Your tongue is heavenly."

His hands went to my hair, gently pushing more of himself into me.

As a twenty-five-year-old woman, this wasn't the first time I'd had a man in my mouth. But Callum filled me in ways I didn't know were possible. It made me wonder what it would be like to have him inside my pussy.

I heated at the thought and picked up my pace, licking

and lapping, sustaining a frantic rhythm to bring him to release in my mouth.

My mind raced as fast as my heart. What would he taste like? Would he want me to swallow? Probably. My mouth watered at the thought, making his cock slide smooth and easy as he jerked and hardened inside me.

"Robin!" he roared in a hellish voice I barely recognized. I felt his muscles flexing and throbbing as he jerked violently in his chair. His hand gripped my hair and ripped my mouth off him, making a wet popping sound as he broke from the suction of my lips.

"Get out!"

I blinked. What had I done? Then it dawned on me. He was sweating buckets, and his chest was rising and falling heavily in rapid succession. The tendons in his neck were stretched taut.

He was about to shift.

Callum wasn't going to let me see his true form, he never did.

"Sir, please let me stay—"

"OUT!" The angel burst out of his chair, making me stumble backward. His body was swelling as his muscles expanded, and the seams of his charcoal-gray suit split as it struggled to cover his growing physique.

He spun around, hiding himself so I couldn't see. "Get the fuck out!"

I ran for the door as fast as I could with tears burning my eyes. In the last glimpse I got of him, I saw him hunched over his desk as white feathers exploded from his back.

Slamming the door behind me, I leaned against it and slid to the floor. My heart pounded with emotion, and my head spun.

In three years, we'd never gotten that close. There'd been plenty of flirting. Lots of eye-fucking.

But that? We'd never done that.

I'd been nervous as hell but, now that I'd crossed that line, I wanted to repeat it.

I needed to touch him again. Every time we got closer, I felt this invisible *thing* looming over us. Something big, something monumental.

Too bad he kept pushing me away. What was so horrifying about it that he kicked me out of his office mid blow job?

My mind fumbled with the possibilities. I knew there were supernatural species that were borderline alien with their monstrous features and appendages. But Callum was at least an angel. He'd have a brawny build with wings, and maybe some extra sets of eyes somewhere. I'd be lying if I said I never laid in bed at night, touching myself to the thought of his feathers brushing against my flesh as his celestial eyes bore into me. Would they be blue? Another color?

By his reaction just now, his other half had to be something totally monstrous.

And that excited me. By now, curiosity was eating me alive.

My eyes drifted shut, and I tried to steady my breathing. In his office, kneeling before his spread legs, I'd seen it. That light he kept locked inside himself, like the doves that used to live in that awful cage. Such beauty didn't deserve to be trapped in such a dark place.

Only with Callum, it wasn't so easy to set him free.

A noise carried through the door, and I pressed my ear to the wood to hear better. Grunting. The heavy, barrelling breaths of a man wrapped in pleasure.

Callum was finishing what we'd started.

I should have just gone back to my desk and pretended I hadn't heard anything.

I shouldn't have slipped my hand beneath my skirt and slid my fingers over my wet center. I'd purposely not worn panties today. By Callum's reaction, I'd almost wished I'd done it sooner. His reaction to my scent left me feeling... powerful. Like if I pushed a little bit harder, I really could wrap him around my finger. Even though I was the only human that worked at Cupid Inc., Callum wouldn't expect me to be the mole. We had a connection.

He really believed I was loyal to him. And, in a way, I was, so long as his company wasn't in the equation.

My fingers rubbed frantic circles over my sensitive flesh, my movements growing frantic and desperate, seeking the high of release to chase away the guilt that slowly ebbed its way inside me.

When I heard Callum huff out my name through clenched teeth on the other side of the door, I came undone.

Biting my lip, I swallowed down a cry and slumped against the door, breathless.

There wasn't time to enjoy the last laces of pleasure tingling through me, though, because just then, the phone rang. I jumped in surprise and stumbled to my desk.

I let it ring a few times to collect my breath before answering with a "Callum Revear's office."

"Robin." My stomach twisted at the voice on the line. I'd recognize that gravel-rough tone anywhere. It was the head of Cupid's security team. "Is Mr. Reaver available? I have a lead on the mole."

4

CALLUM

I fucking hated myself for wanting her so badly. I lusted for her to the point of total madness.

She was a human. A fucking *human*!

My father had seen them as nothing more than food, something to fuck and feed on before tossing them aside. But that female had robbed me of my heart from day one.

I'd do anything for her.

She was my weakness and my strength. She was a damn barb in my side, and I'd become addicted to the pain. Seeing Robin smile was the difference between a good day and a shitty one. Which pissed me the fuck off. I was Callum Reaver, son of the infamous fallen angel who'd built this company with nothing but his bare hands, stolen celestial magic and his filthy reputation.

A single human like her shouldn't have been so much as a tick on my radar. But here she was, invading my every thought. I was a slave to her scent, her soft flesh, her sinuous curves.

It bothered me how much I wanted her.

I'd grown bored with my fortune, and Cupid Inc.'s legacy. Bored and spiteful.

I needed more than the bounties reaped from my father's shadow.

A mate. That's what I needed.

It was almost poetic justice that the man who stole hearts on others' accounts didn't have a lover himself.

I stormed over to the bar sitting against the far wall of my office, crushed the cap off a fresh bottle of whiskey by pinching it between my taloned fingertips and guzzled it down like some kind of animal.

A hundred red eyes caught my attention in the mirror mounted over the bar, and I glanced up to look at the reflection of my celestial form.

I was an animal.

Growling, I slammed the bottle into the mirror and shattered it, the eyes embedded in my wings glaring at me through the cracks in the glass.

I dropped my hand to my groin and fisted the base of my cock.

Closing my eyes, I recalled the way her doe eyes had widened at the size of my human cock. How would she react to the monstrosity in my hand now?

I gritted my teeth as I pumped my dick, steeping myself in the fresh memory of her plush lips. Fuck. The way they'd felt, ready to milk me dry. The warmth of her tongue caressing the underside of my shaft. And the way she moaned a little when she'd tasted my pre-cum? The sound would be branded into my brain forever.

I strode back to my desk, and my chair groaned underneath my weight when I collapsed into it. Keeping one hand firmly on my shaft, I logged into my computer and accessed the security cameras. Particularly the feed I visited the most often. It was the one in the hall leading up to my office, with Robin's desk in perfect view.

It wasn't like the camera was a secret, it was clearly mounted for everyone to see. But clearly, Robin had forgotten all about it. That, or she wanted me to see her on the floor with her back propped against my office door and her hand shoved up her skirt.

I let out a low growl as my eyes settled on her lush, milky thighs on full display.

Then, my attention trailed up to her face. Seeing her soft features twisted up in obscene bliss was what pushed me over the edge.

Thick ropes of seed pulsed from my cock, drenching my hand. My head fell back on my chair's headrest as I rode through the waves of pleasure. My meaty hand continued to stroke my length, smearing my seed over the ridged flesh until the entire thing glistened in the dim light of my office.

I stared at her image on my computer screen, watching her hands smear her own arousal over the interior of her thighs. I beat another one out.

My erection wasn't deflating.

Fucking Christ! Curse my incubus blood. This shit was torture.

With a snarl, I slammed my fist into my desk, cracking the wood, and started jacking myself off a third time, hoping round three would quell this feral lust brewing like a storm inside me.

I came again, torrents of hot cum dripping over my knuckles and staining my slacks. It was a good thing I was married to my work, because I had a suite in the next room over with several changes of clothes.

It's not like this was a common occurrence, but it wouldn't be the first time I'd gratified myself to her on the security feed. Usually, she was just working behind her desk, but there were days when the mere sight of her was enough to drive me up a wall.

I sighed, stretching my wings out. It had been some time since I'd shifted. I was careful never to let Robin see me. So when she picked herself up to answer the phone, then walked back to my door, I'd already shifted back.

Seconds later, the light rap of her knuckles sounded. "S-sir? You have a call from your head of security. Should I transfer him to your line?"

Hearing the quiver in her voice, I glanced back at the camera feed. Her demeanor had changed in an instant. Was she crying?

"Did I upset you?"

"No, sir. It's the call. They have a member of the human-rights organization down in the security holding room."

I bristled. She called them human-rights activists. That's what the media called them too. They hadn't shown up until someone internal leaked information about the human trial for the Cupid's Arrow formula.

They weren't human-rights activists.

They were anti-supernatural hatemongers.

"Why the tears? What does that have to do with you?"

A pause. She took a breath. "You're going to hurt them, aren't you?"

Ah, sweet Robin. Her kindness had no business in a place like this. "These people don't deserve your sympathy." I glanced at the cage in the corner of my office, a smile curling at the corner of my mouth. "I think I'm about to take on a new pet. And there will be no setting this one free, little bird."

5

CALLUM

The bastard was tied to a chair in the middle of the room. A bare bulb swayed over his head, casting an ominous shadow over the floor.

His head sagged forward, blood leaking from his broken nose like a faucet. "I don't know anything, you monstrous fuck!"

"You're lying." My tone came out hushed, but packed enough electricity that I could see the goosebumps raise over his flesh from where I leaned against the wall. I took a moment to let him bask in the wake of his fresh bruises as I examined my bloody knuckles.

Torture was a craft, and I was a master artisan. Inflicting pain was easy. It was knowing when to pull punches for the most effect that came with practice.

After giving my captive several minutes to simmer in his own thoughts, I pushed off the wall and slowly prowled toward him. "We're just getting started, so you haven't seen 'monstrous.' Not yet."

Standing in front of him, I stabbed my finger into the bite one of my wolves had left on his arm. My lips twitched into a smirk at his shrill scream.

"You've invoked the ire of a dark angel. And I'm sure there are plenty of rumors flying around in your little hate group regarding my heritage. That I'm half angel, half nightmare. Imagine all the ways I can break your pathetic body. If you can't handle a little wolf bite, you're in for a tough night. So I'll ask you once more. Who among my employees is your contact?"

The human lifted his head, then spat a mouthful of his blood—and a shard of his tooth—in my face.

I didn't flinch. Instead, my smile turned manic, and the color drained from my victim's face.

He was losing his nerve. Good. This whole mole business had gone on for too long. I needed to find the traitor and make

them pay.

"I-I'm not telling you anything. I'm not afraid of you."

I crouched in front of him like an adult would with a young child. "More lies. Because you are going to tell me everything."

I shifted into my angelic form, enjoying the look of horror that washed over him as my shadow swallowed him. My countless red eyes gleamed in the reflection of his own. I extended my wings, wrapping them around him so that all he'd see were white feathers and my bloody-red glare from every angle.

Extending my taloned-tipped fingers, I placed their points around where his heart sat, beating frantically in his chest.

"Human hearts are such fragile things. You know, my father collected hearts. You'd think since he was an angel with the nickname 'Cupid' that he'd collect the hearts of lovers, but no. He collected the hearts of his enemies. Literally. They're sitting up in my suite in a little case."

The man's blood-curdling scream erupted through the

room. Not that it mattered. This room was soundproof. Even if it weren't, no one would dare come to help him. "I think your heart will make a nice addition."

I pushed my talons a little deeper, a bright-red stain spreading, bleeding across the front of his shirt. "And then your confidant's heart can be the second addition."

I paused, giving him one last chance to spill his secrets before ripping his heart from his chest.

The man took several gasping breaths as he tried to get ahold of himself. Then, he lifted his head to lock eyes with my main set. "Yeah? Is that before or after you fuck her?"

The blood in my veins turned ice cold. "What?"

There was a tense pause, then the human sputtered a cruel laugh. "Are you so hard up for your secretary that you're blind? Fucking rich for having so many eyes."

Another pause. All ability to articulate left me as I tried to parse my thoughts. "Are you saying Robin is the mole?"

"How can you be so dense? She's human! You don't think she's actually interested in your freaky monster cock, do you?"

"My secretary has been the one passing information to your organization?" I asked again, not believing what I was hearing.

"Yeah, poor bitch. She's had to get nice and cozy with you so you wouldn't suspect she was the plant. Seeing as she's the only human working for you, she's probably had to lay it on real thick."

Slowly, the ice in my body began to melt as a little flame of rage ignited in my chest, making my blood boil.

It had been Robin the entire time.

I felt so stupid. Of course the thought of her being the mole had occurred to me, but I'd quickly pushed it out of my mind. I didn't think she knew about Cupid's Arrow. Before the leak, that had been a classified project that only the chemistry department, myself and my investors had been privy to.

For three years I'd felt a connection to her.

I thought she'd felt it too. No, I *knew* she had. Stupid me for thinking that it would garner any kind of loyalty.

As the knife in my back sunk deeper, my captive continued his informative boasting.

"Robin's the one that told us about your fucked-up experiments on our kind. We're going to tear your operation down before Cupid's Arrow hits the market."

I stretched to my full height, glaring down at the pathetic sack of flesh I was seconds away from silencing forever. "My love potions have been on the market for years. Billions of dollars in sales, and not a peep from you people. Then, when there's so much as a whisper about a formula in production that *may* work on humans, you're crawling all over me like fucking cockroaches."

"Yeah." He spit out another tooth. "Why would we care about your kind drugging each other? You're animals. You deserve to rip each other apart! But humans? Humans and supernaturals can't be fated mates, or whatever the hell you call it, for a reason. It's unnatural. You freaks will claim and mate our kind over our dead bodies!"

"How fortunate for you," I snarled. "That can be arranged."

"No, plea—" That's all he got out before I plunged my claws into his chest cavity and ripped out his beating heart. I didn't even bother glancing at it before I let it fall to the floor with a sickening *plop*.

I had another heart I was more interested in claiming.

There weren't words to describe the pain from the invisible knife in my fucking back. All this time, she was the mole.

How could I be so... blind?

If my father were here, he'd make some comment about the irony, seeing as I was an angel, and that I was more like my demon mother.

I pushed thoughts of my parents away and focused my rage on Robin, and what I was going to do to her as retribution for her betrayal.

If I were any other boss, I'd fire her.

But I was Callum Reaver, the beating heart of Cupid Inc. Firing her would be too easy. She deserved a slow, painful punishment.

I would invade her every cell. I'd make her want me. I'd make her hate to want me. And I was going to do that by doing what I'd been too kind to do before.

I was going to make her mine forever.

Reaching into my shirt pocket, I pulled out my cell and tapped at the screen, leaving bloody fingerprints all over the device. Placing it to my ear, it rang once before my head of chemistry answered.

"Mix me a bottle of Cupid's Arrow and have it delivered to security."

"But, sir, that hasn't been properly tested yet. Unless you found us a test bunny?"

I felt a malevolent grin creep across my face. "Not a bunny. A little bird."

6

ROBIN

I couldn't bring myself to run.

It would be pointless. Callum was rich and had the resources to track me down. At least, that's what I told myself. In truth, there was a part of me that felt like I deserved whatever punishment my boss had in store.

From my phone call with security, I knew they'd found my contact. There was no doubt in my mind that Callum would crack him open and spill out all his secrets—*my* secret. Probably by physically ripping him open with his bare hands. Once he discovered I was the traitor, he'd probably tear me apart piece by piece too. Only with me, he'd tease it out. He'd make it last.

No matter how brutal the punishment was, there was some other dark part of me that wanted this. Geez. When did I get so twisted?

So I sat at my desk, and I waited for Callum to return.

I tried my best to get back to work by going through my emails, but I couldn't focus.

All I could think about was what Callum Reaver was going to do to me.

I wondered if he was going to give me a chance to explain

myself. Would he think that I'd been a mole for all three years of my employment? Would he let me explain that I'd only been working with them for six months, shortly after I'd stumbled across the files for the Cupid's Arrow project? Even if I was able to explain, would he care? What did it matter if I was loyal to him for two and a half years, only to betray him in the end?

As the minutes crawled by on their hands and knees, my nerves started to fray.

Maybe I still had time to escape...

My heart slammed painfully into my ribs, its rapid-fire beat falling in line with the heavy footsteps of Callum's expensive Italian shoes against the marble floors.

He came into view a second later, his sea-blue eyes drilling straight through me, stabbing straight into my lungs like twin daggers.

I couldn't breathe.

"S-sir." I stood up and had to brace my hand against my desk to keep my noodley legs from giving out.

Callum appeared in his human form, just as he always did when I was around. But even if he appeared mortal, I wasn't fooled by the facade. He had the imposing aura of a dark angel, with or without wings.

Especially now.

He was splattered head to toe in bright red, his Armani suit ruined. Even if the blood stains were removable, the expensive three-piece suit wasn't salvageable due to the rips at the seams. Patches of his skin peeked through the damaged fabric, and what little remained of my breath latched in my throat. I could just make out the ink. I didn't know he had tattoos. I found my mind drifting, imagining what his fit physique looked like all wrapped in dark swaths of ink.

Shit. What was *wrong* with me? I should have been

worrying about what he was going to do to me now that he'd discovered I was the mole, not thinking about what his tatted body looked like naked!

My entire world turned sideways and ceased to make sense when Callum smoothed a bloody hand over his slicked-back hair and smiled at me. "Care to join me for a drink, Robin?"

I blinked rapidly. Why wasn't he mad? Maybe my contact hadn't cracked, or maybe they'd gotten the wrong guy. Very few people in the anti-sup organization knew that I worked for Cupid. I allowed myself to hope that my cover remained intact for at least a little while longer.

Callum stepped around my desk and took my hand in his. "Sweet little bird, you're shaking like a leaf. What's got you so worked up?"

"You're covered in blood..." My voice wavered when I noticed something in his free hand. His smile stretched wide when he saw me take notice of it, and he tossed it on my desk.

It was a human heart. So much for that poor bastard.

"It isn't the first time you've seen me like this. It's never put you off before."

It was true. This wasn't the first time he'd left his office for a lunch meeting, or to check up on one of the departments, only to return covered in blood.

This was the first time he'd come back with a freaking heart though. Shit.

Callum's smile grew bitter, and his grip on my hand tightened. "Perhaps it's because the last time you saw me like this, I had just killed an unhinged supernatural I caught stealing from me. You didn't so much as bat a pretty eyelash at that, most likely because they weren't human."

I didn't miss the edge in his voice. He released my hand and opened the door to his office. "Now, join me for that drink? I think we could both use one after the day we've had."

I followed Callum through his office and into his private suite through the back door hidden around the corner from the bar. He had a penthouse apartment downtown, but he rarely went there; he practically lived at work. My heart started to beat faster the second I stepped into the main living area of the suite. I'd never been back here before.

Until today, he'd always taken care to keep the professional boundary between us drawn, even if we both danced too close to the line from time to time. His apartment was completely off-limits.

"This is beautiful, sir." To say his view was breathtaking was a bit of an understatement. The apartment had floor-to-ceiling windows and, considering that we were on the top floor of Cupid Inc., we had a dazzling view of the city.

"Yes, beautiful," he murmured, not taking his eyes off me.

The rest of his living space was modern, decorated in posh furniture and art that probably cost more than what I made in a month. There was a kitchen in the far corner of the room with marble finishes and stainless steel, state-of-the-art appliances. "Your kitchen looks like it's never been used."

"It hasn't. You know I don't eat." I glanced back to find him behind the bar to the left of the living room. This bar was smaller than the one in his office, but it had more personality than everything else in the space. There was a huge cabinet pushed up against the wall, the shelves lined with mirrors that displayed a colorful array of liquor bottles, and a bunch of odds and ends to feast my eyes on. I approached the bar and took a seat on the stool as I took in every piece.

"But you drink." My eyes went back to him, finding him fixing us both an Old Fashioned.

"I drink," he confirmed in a dry tone. "I suppose I inherited both my father's company and his affinity for liquor. Those, and all this shit." He jerked his head toward the cabinet of curiosities.

My attention went back to the items. Callum never talked about his father. I studied the trinkets and trophies more carefully. "What's in the wooden boxes?"

"The hearts of Cupid's enemies."

I gave an awkward laugh, but the sound died in my chest when I caught Callum's sharp look and realized he was being serious. "That would explain the heart you brought back from your, erm, meeting. A new addition to the collection, I guess."

"That was a gift," he muttered. There was a strange bend to his tone that had my thighs clenching.

I swallowed, shifting my gaze to the arrow mounted on the wall above the cabinet. "Your dad really loved the whole Cupid gimmick, didn't he?"

"Of course. He basically was Cupid. When he was younger, his job was to help determine which supernatural creatures would be fated to one another. Though, there was no shooting of arrows or any of the other crap you see in old cartoons. It was mostly just paperwork."

I perked up at this new information. "Wait, really? So he was like a matchmaker for supernaturals?"

Callum nodded.

I took a breath, gathering the nerve to fire off the question burning on my tongue. "Why did he start this company?"

"He was fired from using the angel magic as it was intended, so he was kicked out of Heaven." His brows furrowed into a scowl. "If that's what you want to call it. And his magical abilities were stripped from him. So, he started this company, using his powers through other means. He figured out a way to brew his magic and place it in bottles.

Then, he made the potions available to anyone who desired his services. It was his 'fuck you' to his people."

"Why was he fired?"

Shadows cut across Callum's face with his scowl. "He used his magic to choose a mate for himself."

"Angels aren't supposed to take a mate?"

"It's not that. It's who he selected for a mate. My mother was..." His voice trailed off. "They saw her as an abomination. We'll just leave it at that. That's enough questions."

My lips slashed with a frown. Something was off. He wasn't usually so short with me, and he was never this open about his parents.

I was still aching to know what kind of supernatural his mother was. There were rumors about Callum not being a full-blooded angel, and he'd just confirmed it. He was a hybrid. That tracked. I knew there was something about his true form that he was hiding from me. Whatever his mother had been, he was either ashamed... or he was just trying to keep me safe.

"T-thank you for telling me that. I'm sure it's not easy talking about it, but—"

"Don't do that."

I stared at him for a beat, taken aback by the sudden way he'd cut me off. "Don't do what?"

"Don't fucking thank me." He refused to look me in the eye. His movements were tight, and he was tenser than I'd ever seen him. He mixed our drinks like he was on a mission. When he took our glasses and ducked behind the bar, it dawned on me that he was.

Through the mirrored shelving, I could see him add two twists of orange rinds, one to each glass. Then he took out two bottles from his pocket. He moved so fast, if I'd blinked I would have missed it.

He emptied the contents of the black vial over his. Then the white vial over mine.

Stuffing the now-empty bottles back in his pocket, he brought the glasses to the bar surface and topped them each with a bright-red maraschino cherry.

The icing on the poison.

I tried to keep my face emotionless, but it was almost an impossible task as I felt the cold and clammy hand of fear grip my heart and squeeze.

He'd just spiked our drinks.

The black and white twin bottles weren't the regular love potions we sold. Those were pink and purple bottles. Purple for the consumer, and pink for the intended mate. If they had been pink and purple, I wouldn't have cared. They didn't work on humans. But the black and white bottles? I'd seen those in the classified files for Cupid's Arrow.

These were the love potions that had been specially formulated for humans.

It was almost funny how such tiny bottles had created this entire mess. The entire reason I was in this position was because I'd wanted to stop the human experiments that were going on to test this very formula.

It had backfired. Big time. Because now I was the guinea pig. Though I couldn't help but feel that this was karma for betraying Callum.

I lifted my gaze and, for the first time since entering the suite, he looked me in the eye. And he saw the tears pouring down my cheeks.

He knew I was the mole.

I picked up the glass, trying to keep my cool.

Callum's glower sharpened, and my chest ached with the hurt I saw etched into his gorgeous face. He probably thought he was doing a good job hiding his emotions from me, but I could see past the mask.

"Drink it, little bird."

I looked into the glass, my thoughts and emotions running riot. If I drank it, I'd be saving other humans from trial tests. But if it worked, then the formula would hit the market, and then any supernatural could waltz into a drug store and... I swallowed. It was a double-edged sword. I'd be saving my kind from suffering now, only so more could be hurt later.

More tears trailed down my cheeks and peppered the countertop around my glass. I wasn't crying because that notion scared me. I was crying because my heart already belonged to him, with or without the potion.

I hated that the thing finally bringing us together was the knife that I'd stabbed into his back.

The truth was, I was in love with Callum Reaver. I had been for three years.

And I'd let my hatred for his company get in the way of that.

I deserved this. I deserved to have him, and I deserved for it to hurt.

So I reached out for my glass, brought it to my lips and drained every drop of liquid.

Whether Cupid's Arrow "worked" or not didn't matter at this point. With or without the potion, Callum already owned me. Heart, body and soul.

And the time had come for him to finally claim them, however he saw fit.

7

CALLUM

I took another sip of my drink, not that I needed to. One drop was all it took. "Did you not think I was going to find out eventually?" I asked coolly.

I didn't need to elaborate, she knew what I was talking about.

Her fear was so palpable, I could taste it.

Good.

I wanted to see her shake. That would be a good start.

Then I'd make her fucking scream.

Maybe I was more like my father than I thought. The anger siphoning through my body was normal. This side of me was my father coming through, and I usually did well at repressing it. It had always been there, though, lurking beneath my surface. Which was exactly why I'd kept her at a distance. I'd always known if she got too close, I'd hurt her.

But in the last hour, the circumstances had changed. My anger had grown into something dark and dangerous, like a fire that wouldn't be easily sated.

Now I *wanted* to hurt her. Break her. Pluck out her heart and mount it amongst my father's collection. *No. Not that.* That would be a waste of my new mate.

My new pet.

"You're going to regret what you've done," I warned her with an icy smile. "I'm going to put you in a cage."

Her eyes widened, and her fingers trembled around her glass. "What?"

"Don't worry. In about ten minutes, the potion will kick in. Once it does, you'll find my punishments more appealing."

"Cupid's Arrow," she said in a breathless whisper.

"Yes, little bird. Almost ironic, isn't it?"

I'd anticipated her fear, hoped for it even. What I didn't expect was another familiar fragrance I'd come to know all too well.

Fuck me. There was some part of her that wanted this.

Robin was turned on by the idea of being mine. Which was absolutely fucked, considering she was a part of the anti-supernatural group who loathed my kind. Maybe her attempts at seducing me hadn't been just an act to keep me close and blissfully unaware.

So my little bird had a masochistic streak in her.

This was going to be *fun.*

"I'm sorry," she said, her songbird voice quivering with the fresh wave of tears that flowed down her flushed cheeks.

Christ, why did she have to be so goddamn beautiful when she cried?

My eyes narrowed. "If you were sorry, you wouldn't have betrayed me."

"I really am sorry, sir! I never meant to hurt you. But your company is evil..."

I slammed my fist into my bar, glasses and liquor bottles rattling dangerously. "I am my company! I am Cupid Inc.!"

She hopped off her stool and flung herself against my chest in a fit of sobs, craning her neck to look up at me through her wet lashes.

Either she was a very good actress or there was a part of her that truly regretted her betrayal. No matter what, I'd make her regret it.

"You are not Cupid, Callum! You are not your father; there is good in you!"

I gritted my teeth, hating how much hearing my first name on her lips turned me on. My cock was swelling, and I felt my celestial senses take over. If I got much more worked up than this, I'd shift. Suddenly, I didn't care so much about her seeing me in my true form. I wanted her to quake in fear before me, and witness the living, breathing monstrosity that lurked beneath my surface.

"You're right. There was good inside me, but you set that free today, just like my father's birds when you started working for me three years ago. I thought..."

Hating how vulnerable I felt in this moment, I couldn't bring myself to finish the thought. I loved this little human or, at least, I loved her as much as a monster like me could.

I'd been stupid to think that in some small way, she loved me too.

"I thought we had a connection."

"We do." Her tears flowed freely now. She looked so heartbroken. She was probably just trying to save her own hide by manipulating me. Too bad pulling on my heartstrings wasn't going to work. My heart was broken.

I seized her wrist, gripping it hard enough to leave bruises. She winced, but didn't pull away. "Do we? Is that why you joined those xenophobes?"

She blinked. "Xenophobes?"

"Supernatural racists, Robin! Don't play dumb!" I roared at her, making her flinch. "They hate my kind! They'd sooner see us all burn to ash before swallowing the idea that in the coming years, interspecies mating will become mainstream."

"N-no! I didn't join them. I just told them about the Cupid's Arrow project. I didn't like that you were keeping humans like lab rats. It was sick! I wanted to put a stop to it. I want to put a stop to the entire company and all its wickedness! So I went to the people who I knew would stir up a media nightmare. Slowly losing sales was the gentlest way of shutting you down."

"By slowly suffocating me?"

"It was either that or taking a match and lighter fluid to the place," she snapped, a spark of defiance lighting up her green eyes. Gods, I loved that little rebellious streak in her. Even when I was fuming.

"I don't care that you're an angel, Callum. Your wings don't bother me. I know…"

I shook her, trying to knock whatever words she was going to say out of her. My patience was a fraying rope, and we were on the last strand. I was about to snap. "You know what?"

"I know you're a hybrid. Whatever it is that you are, I don't care."

"You're lying."

She raised her chin, her green gaze narrowing into slits. "I'm not lying! I like the idea of seeing exactly what you are. After all these years, I still haven't seen the real you. You're the one who decided I would be disgusted. You never gave me an opportunity to accept that side of you."

The things I would give for her words to be true. I'd trade my whole damn fortune. I'd pluck out my own wings feather by feather. I'd burn down everything my father and I had built over the years for her to truly accept me. But even if she accepted my angel blood, she still didn't know that I was a sex demon. A sadist. A monster.

But… maybe she wouldn't reject me. She was right, I hadn't given her an opportunity to accept me for what I was.

I couldn't resist anymore.

Taking a step back, I shredded the destroyed suit jacket and collared shirt from my body, baring my torso to her.

Her eyes were as wide as dinner plates, and the scent of her arousal grew stronger as she drank in my muscled physique. Twin stains of pink blotted her cheeks as her gaze found the tattoo covering my heart. Ironically, it was of an anatomically correct heart with an arrow piercing it at an angle. It was a little on the nose, but I'd gotten it the day after my father died. Emotions had been running high that day.

There was the unsettling sound of snapping bones as my body made way for four wings that sprouted from my shoulder blades. Pressure built in my skull before the points of my black horns exploded to the surface. My nails elongated into deadly talons and, all at once, my celestial eyes blinked open.

"You accept me?" I rumbled in the hellish baritone native to this form. "Then kiss me."

8

ROBIN

The visage of the dark angel before me was more demonic than every nightmare I'd ever had combined, yet somehow I wasn't afraid. I was awestruck.

He had four wings, two on each side, covered in snow-white feathers and red, beady eyes that drilled right through me.

I found myself so enamored by each one that I couldn't move. It's not that they disgusted me, it was the opposite. I was frozen where I stood, initially shocked.

He was beautiful, terrifyingly so.

Something not far off the mark from inadequacy swept through me, robbing all the confidence out of my sails.

How could someone as awe-inspiring and powerful as this male want me? I was a human. There was a reason why so many people believed that humans and supernaturals couldn't become mates. They could fuck, but they couldn't seal the mating bond. And that was because there was no record of it ever happening.

And now it all made sense.

He was a god, and I was nothing.

I couldn't move. It was like his eyes were a thousand little needles, pinning me down. I was so lost in their gaze that I barely registered the fact that he was talking to me. I managed to jerk my attention from the sea of feathers and eyes, only for his horns to snag my focus.

He had fucking horns!

They were black, and just thick enough to wrap my fingers around so their tips would meet on the other side. They sprouted from his temples and curved backwards, following the flow of his slicked-back hair.

He was a shock to the senses, nightmarish and mouthwatering all at once. Each detail of his celestial form gripped me by the fucking throat and made it impossible to breathe.

What was he trying to tell me? By the time I'd shaken myself from my awestruck haze, he was dragging me out of his suite and back into his office by my arm.

His rage was so palpable that I could taste it in my mouth, as bitter as ash.

"I'm s-sorry, what?"

He said nothing as he wrenched me into the next room.

I didn't expect us to have company. There was a man I recognized from maintenance, a vampire from the night shift, inside the floor-to-ceiling cage in the corner of the room. He was installing something, by the looks of things. He scrambled up when he saw Callum approach. Hastily picking up his tool box, he refused to look his superior in any of his eyes and instead kept his line of sight glued to his feet. "Chain's been installed, sir."

Chain?

Callum dismissed the vampire, and he left, leaving me alone with the demonic angel once more.

All the air left my lungs when I registered the huge coil of chain lying on the floor inside the cage. One end was secured around one of the bars, and on the other end of it was a large metal cuff. No, not a cuff.

A collar.

I saw where this was going. And maybe the potion was starting to work, because I felt conflicted. Which was crazy. I should have been freaking out, and I was. But why was I so hot? I was blushing—full body—as if it were his bed he was planning on chaining me to instead of a cage.

A fucking cage.

Like I was some kind of naughty animal that needed to be locked away.

The cage hadn't held anything for years. It was clean, and large enough for me to walk around in. He couldn't really be planning on keeping me there, could he? And if he did, for how long? It's not like anyone would come looking for me. I didn't have anyone else outside this company. The only people who'd wonder what happened would be the acquaintances I'd made among the anti-sups, and they'd probably figured this would happen to me sooner rather than later.

From what everyone knew of Cupid's CEO, no one would expect to see me again.

He guided me to the cage, and I didn't struggle.

Could Cupid's Arrow be working? Were my mind, body and soul being chemically altered like the potion claimed?

No. I was already in love with Callum. I didn't feel any different, other than the spike of adrenaline racing through my bloodstream.

I'd always suspected I had a bit of a masochistic streak, but I'd only had short flings and one-night stands before. I'd never felt secure enough to explore my kinkier side with strangers.

So the cage didn't bother me as Callum probably hoped it would.

Curiosity was my guiding light now.

Callum was so massive in this form that he took up almost the entire space, forcing me to shuffle close to the bars. His wings swept against me. His feathers were softer than I imagined. Goosebumps prickled my arms, and his eyes suddenly captured mine.

Oh my gods. His feathers had sensation; they had to be crazy sensitive to pick up on the tiny bumps. Looking into his many eyes, I found myself more curious than transfixed. Sure, he was still massive and frightening to look at with his horns and his soul-piercing red glare, but I found my mind wondering what it might be like to mate with a creature like this.

The only sexual encounters I'd had—my moment with Cal notwithstanding—were with my vanilla boyfriends and hookups. So it went without saying that they were human men.

Getting pushed up against these bars and taking whatever Callum was hiding in his slacks would be an experience like no other.

My lungs slammed together when the angel crouched in front of me. His wings were in the way, so I couldn't see what he was doing. Instead of wrenching my skirt up like I hoped, though, the metallic clink of chain sounded as he slowly stretched back to his full height.

On the next breath, there was the cold bite of metal against my throat as he secured the collar around my neck.

Oh, gods. This was really happening.

I tried and failed to calm my breathing, and my palms began to sweat. My mind fractured in half as I tried to parse my current reality. I really was Callum's little bird. He wasn't going to let me go; he was going to make my punishment last. He'd tease it out to my last breath.

And still, I wanted this. I *deserved* this. He wasn't a good man, and that's why I'd betrayed him. But I found myself caring less and less about that. He'd been good to *me*. That's what should have mattered.

I would never regret saving those humans, but I did regret how I went about it.

He gave a testing tug to the chain that rested between my breasts.

"The potion will take effect in a matter of minutes, and all this will be much more pleasant. Until then, calm down. Otherwise, you're going to pass out."

"How can I calm down? You put a collar on me."

"Think of it as an early Valentine's Day gift. A pretty necklace for my pretty traitor."

"What are you going to do to me?"

He reached up, his massive hand closing around my throat over the collar. My pussy clenched at the possessive gesture. "I'm going to make you *mine*."

9

ROBIN

"There's no bed in here. Where am I supposed to sleep?" I asked from the cage, leaning so my cheeks pressed between the bars.

Callum sat at his desk, shirtless and still in his angelic form, staring at his computer screen. It was getting late, and nothing had happened yet... well, apart from the whole drugging me thing and the locking me in a cage thing. Aside from that, he was the perfect gentleman.

How messed up was it that I was almost disappointed?

After he'd put the collar on me, I'd expected him to follow through on some of his dark threats. After dropping that casual *"I'm going to make you mine,"* he'd charged out of my cage and planted himself in his chair for a late-night work sesh.

What in the actual fuck was happening? Did I live here now? Did I still work for him?

Was he going to rail me to death or not?

"The chain is long enough for you to reach every room in the suite," he said without glancing up from his computer.

"Just the one bed?"

"We're mates now. Get used to the idea of sleeping in my bed."

"Just because you spiked my drink and chained me up doesn't make me your mate. You're going to have to fuck me to seal the mating bond."

He finally glanced up, shooting me a glare through my prison bars. "Don't preach to me about the mating bond, little bird. I was practically there when that magic was written."

"You're not that old."

"I'm almost that old. Does that bother you?"

He paused, then typed away at his keyboard.

"What are you writing?"

"Your responses. Your reaction. You are the final case study for Cupid's Arrow. Everything you do, I will be studying for side effects for the next twenty-four hours. After the twenty-four-hour period, I'll send your results to the lab and the formula will be in its final phase before it goes to mass production."

"Tomorrow? But that's Valentine's Day."

His lips twitched into an almost smile. "Poetic, isn't it?"

"You can't be serious about putting this on the market."

Callum's expression darkened, and all the pupils on his wings shrunk into malevolent slits. "That's where you're wrong. I'm deadly serious."

"Why? So you're not a saint. You like ripping the hearts out of xenophobes and chaining your staff to the creepy cage you keep in your office. But you're not evil. The love potions, Cupid's Arrow, those were your father's ideas. Why are you so obsessed with keeping it all going?"

The dark angel shot to his feet, his four wings expanding all around him. I found myself stepping backward as far as the cage would allow me as he strode toward me.

Imposing. Baleful. Noxiously ethereal. But I was picking

up on something else from him, something more subtle. Despair. Desperation to be understood.

He gripped the bars, pushing his face against the metal. "Because it's all I have left!"

There it was. Finally. The truth.

Callum Reaver was upholding Cupid Inc.'s dark legacy because he wanted something to hold on to.

I forced my feet forward, ignoring the instinctual urge to shy away from his eyes. Approaching the cage, I brushed my fingers over his fists that were still clenched around the bars. "That's not true. You have me."

His hand shot through the cage, taking hold of the chain and yanking it, forcing me against the cold metal. He brought his mouth to the shell of my ear, sneering. "I have you because I'm forcing you to be mine."

Fresh tears rolled from my eyes. I was crying, not from fear, but because all I felt was sadness for Callum Reaver.

"You could have had me before, you know."

"I'm sure," he scoffed. "That's why you joined an anti-supernatural hate group."

"I don't hate supernaturals. I've worked for you for three years, sir. I only started leaking info to them six months ago, as soon as I learned about Cupid's Arrow."

His fists clenched tighter around the chain, knuckles paling. "You didn't bat an eye at the supernatural testing."

"I did, actually. I originally got a job here because I wanted to find a way to stop what was going on. Maybe not completely, but in a small part. But then I met you and I..."

"You what?"

Fell in love, I wanted to say. "I changed my mind. You took over for your father and I saw that you were better than him. You were still pushing out the product, but at least you disbanded a lot of the unethical methods of testing and producing the love potions. Then, when I found out about Cupid's Arrow... I was mad, so I attended a couple of the anti-sup rallies. I thought it was the best way to disband the trial testing. But you know what I think? I don't think you halted testing on it because of bad publicity and the lack of funding the protests brought on. I think you did it because you care more about humans than your father did."

Callum's presence darkened, sucking all the warmth out of the room. "And why would I care about humans?"

"Because *I'm* human. You don't want to hurt me. Not really. You've always wanted to keep me safe. Especially from you."

"You've cured me of that kindness," he growled. "Now I don't care if I break you."

I lifted my chin, tamping down on my nerves. "Then break me. Do your study trials on me. Do whatever the hell you want. I already got the two things I wanted."

His nostrils flared. "And what is that?"

"The first is that Cupid's Arrow isn't going to go to market. You won't let it. You'll do the right thing in the end."

He rocked back on his feet, all of his eyes raking over me, making me feel naked and exposed. I didn't hate the sensation.

"And the second thing you wanted?"

I chewed my lower lip. "You, Callum."

10

CALLUM

The formula was working, but not in the way I'd expected it to. She wanted me, that much was clear. But she wasn't acting the same way the other humans had in the early trial studies. They had been compliant and pliable.

I still felt that pull to seal the mating bond, but Robin had her own will, and that little defiant flame within her burned as bright as ever. The only difference now was that her filter had come off and she was saying all the things she'd already known, but had been too afraid to say.

At the end of the day, I didn't give a fuck about Cupid's Arrow hitting the market.

This was about her and me.

"You want me, little bird?"

She gave a little nod, the chain around her neck clinking with the movement.

"Then get on your knees and take me out. I want you to see what you're about to get fucked with."

Her arousal instantly spiked the air, making every muscle in my body wind tight in anticipation. I fought the impulse to rip the cage door off its hinges and bury myself in her soft pussy right here and now.

I watched as she lowered herself to her knees, her hands shaking as she fumbled with my fly. She was eager, but nervous. She'd already seen my dick, but that was in my human form. It was bigger than most, but it was still just a dick. My cock in my shifted form was a whole different ball game, as the humans said.

"That's it, little bird," I cooed, my hand slipping through the bars to gently grip her bun on the top of her head while my other hand maintained a loose hold on her metal leash. My gentle encouragement seemed to ease her nerves. She stopped shaking, and her fingers seemed more sure of themselves as she pulled out my erection, along with my heavy set of balls.

I almost came from the look on her face. Her heartbeat launched into hyper speed at the sight of my incubus cock.

"Relax," I told her through a wicked smirk. "It doesn't bite."

"Your mom was a demon." She lifted her head, her wide eyes meeting mine. "She was a—"

"Succubus," I finished for her. "So yes. I am a dark angel, which is just an angel hybrid. But I am the only known half angel, half sex demon. At least that I know of."

Her hands smoothed over my flesh as they explored every inch of me. Her lips puckered, and her scent grew stronger.

She was pleased with what she saw, so the potion had to be working to some extent. Without it, I was certain she'd be put off by my cock with its many bumps and ridges, and intimidating size.

She most certainly wouldn't be drooling like she was now.

Her fingers slid beneath the shaft, feeling out the swell

beneath, and the series of bumps flanking each side. A tiny gasp left her when her fingertips came to the six dull spikes running over the seam between my balls. "Those won't hurt you," I found myself saying. "They'll just provide sensation."

"You don't have to worry about me being scared," she told me, taking me by surprise. "You always thought I'd be too afraid or horrified by your true form. But I'm not." Her breathing picked up more when she dropped her attention back to my cock, lashes fluttering as she gave it a testing pump, earning herself a bead of pre-cum that oozed slowly from the tip.

"Catch it," I said, giving a slight yank on her chain.

Without any hesitation, she stuck out her tongue and caught the bead of milky fluid. My dick twitched.

"That's a good girl," I praised her. "Now show me how good your pretty human lips look wrapped around my monster cock."

She squirmed, but didn't disobey. Her lips puckered and she kissed the tip of me, the point of her tongue swirling over my swollen head. I canted my hips against the bars, thrusting more of me into her cell. Like a good little pet, she took what I offered and pushed as much of me into her mouth as she could fit. It wasn't enough.

"Let's see how good you are at taking your new mate's cock. I think I'll break in this hole first."

My long fingers sunk deeper into her hair. Tugging on both her leash and the back of her head, I pushed my cock deep into her throat. She whimpered around me, making me grow harder and thicker.

"Relax," I told her again. "Just focus on my eyes."

I chuckled when her gaze flickered between my celestial eyes, not sure which ones to focus on. I pumped into her with a steady pace. Christ, she felt good. Hot, wet. All mine.

"You're doing so well," I told her. She swirled her tongue over my ridges, and I clenched my jaw, biting back a moan. Fuck, I wasn't going to last much longer. As I thrust harder and faster, a single tear slid down her cheek.

That was my undoing.

I yanked out of her, pumping my own shaft at a furious pace. "Open your mouth," I demanded on a broken breath. She did as she was told just before thick ropes of cum spurted over her tongue, her flushed cheeks, her nose and some even got in her hair. I made a mess all over her.

She was panting hard, her little body shaking so sweetly for me.

"Swallow," I instructed her.

11

ROBIN

He tasted salty. Forbidden. And something else I couldn't put my finger on. Whatever it was, it was addictive, awakening a ferocious lust inside me I hadn't known was possible.

This wasn't the effect of the potion, I knew that much. If it were, I would have felt its effects earlier. Maybe this was just the work of his incubus cum. I'd heard sex-demon spunk had an aphrodisiac effect. Then again, I'd always been this desperate for him.

So that's what Callum had been hiding from me all these past years. He was half angel, half incubus. His cock wasn't scary or horrifying at all. It was a little intimidating, with its bumps and ridges and—I gulped—spikes. But the look and feel and taste of it ignited that little flame of curiosity into a full-blown forest fire of unbridled desire.

And for some reason it seemed...familiar? No, that was impossible. I pushed the thought from my mind and returned to the moment.

"I want to feel it inside me," I told him, unable to control my emotions for a second longer. "Fuck me, Callum. Please. Make me your mate."

At first, he seemed surprised by my eagerness, then a smug smirk spread across his face.

He probably thought it was the potion at work, but I knew it was something else. Right now, though, I didn't care what it was. I felt myself falling toward Callum Reaver, hard and fast.

The collision was going to be catastrophic, and it made me feel alive. For the first time, I felt safe and free to explore this hidden side of myself.

All of Callum's eyes glazed over with something dark and wicked, leaving my body in a cold sweat. "Get up," he said in a rough voice.

I did as I was told, feeling my head spin as I pushed to my feet. He opened the door to my cage, and the next thing I knew, I was in his arms. He carried me through the suite and into his bathroom. My heart thudded heavily as he removed our clothes. He peeled off my shirt, my skirt and my bra. Then he removed his slacks, letting them fall to the floor.

But despite that, this moment felt… different. Sexually charged, sure. But it felt intimate, romantic almost, even with the collar and the chain—which he left on.

Callum pulled out each pin in my hair, undoing my bun so that my hair flowed down to my hips, then he lifted me onto the edge of the countertop with my back facing the mirror.

"Wait here. I'm going to get something," he murmured before turning and leaving the room for just a moment. I started breathing harder, my belly twisting and tightening. What was he getting?

Callum returned a minute later with a case in hand. He laid it out on the counter beside me and, with a taloned thumb, flicked the clasps loose. The case sprang open, and I found myself looking at a collection of vibrators I was all too familiar with. Cupid Inc. advertised itself as a "love solutions" company for supernaturals. Love potions to capture a mate weren't the only product it offered. Cupid also manufactured an extensive catalog of unconventional sex toys. Tentacle toys, minotaur and dragon dildos, alien ovipositors with silicone kegel eggs... the list went on.

This was the demon collection of vibrators.

"Spread your legs."

I parted my thighs, the cold marble stinging my skin. The chill disappeared when he came closer, standing between my parted thighs with his erect cock inches away from my open center.

His hand hovered over the collection of demon dildos and, a little to my disappointment, opted for the smallest one. "Why can't you fuck me with your dick?"

"Because I'll tear you open if I do that. We have to get your tight little pussy ready to take me. Your body belongs to me now, and I'm going to have fun with it for a very long time. So I'm going to take care of it as best I can. Can't have you breaking on me before I've had my fill of you."

I swallowed thickly and spread myself wide, giving him full access to my center. "Alright."

"First, I want you to touch yourself. Like you did earlier today when you thought I wasn't looking."

What? He'd seen me? How—oh shit. The security cameras. "H-how often have you watched me work?"

"Almost every fucking day since you started working for me. But that was the first time I've ever gotten a show quite like that. Now that I've answered one of your questions, answer one of mine. How many times after work—after all the flirting, all your failed seduction attempts— have you gone home and touched yourself to the thought of me?"

"I'm not sure. A lot..."

A sabulous purr rumbled up from his chest. "Show me

how damn good your fingers look stuffed inside your pretty little cunt."

My whole body fluttered as I reached down, my fingers slipping through my folds. The first few seconds were tense and awkward, but only because I wasn't used to a man watching me with such ferocious interest.

In this moment, though, I felt like I was his entire world.

His name fell from my lips on a moan as my fingers swirled around my clit, teasing my flesh. I dipped a finger inside my entrance, then pulled it back out, spreading my slickness around.

I hadn't been lying to Callum when I'd told him I wasn't sure how many times I'd gone home after work and touched myself to the thought of him. It wasn't like I'd been counting, but even if I had kept a tally, I would have lost it by now.

The image of my boss's dark smirk had been permanently branded into my mind, and self-indulgence to the mere thought of it was almost a nightly occurrence.

What differed was doing it on his bathroom vanity with him looming over me, watching me with his many eyes.

Overwhelmed by the attention, I clamped my own eyes shut and focused on the sensation. I leaned back, my head resting against the mirror's smooth surface. "Fuck, Callum!"

I was so lost in the sensation, pouring my imagination into pretending it was his fingers on my pussy, that I almost jumped out of my skin when a gentle whirring sound buzzed in my ear, joining my fingers on my clit.

"Easy, pet," Callum hushed. His palm slid beneath the chain to flatten against my tummy, the gesture sweet and soothing, while his other hand held the vibrator to my core. Crap, I'd almost forgotten the smallest toy in the demon collection—the one shaped to model an imp cock—was a bullet vibrator, and a damn powerful one at that.

The lowest setting was a lot, but damn it was good. I writhed under Callum's palm while he held me down. His brows furrowed, and his jaw set. He had that same focus he applied to his most intensive work.

His face was still smeared with flecks of my contact's blood, which heightened the sinful, depraved pleasure of it all.

He pushed the vibrator inside me, just a few inches, then threw it down on a hand towel he'd laid out and opted for the size up.

He fucked me with it until I was panting, dangerously close to climax. Just as I was about to come, he yanked it out of me and selected the largest toy in the collection.

I knew this one. I knew it well.

"The Incubus." He showed me the toy with a flourish, turning it this way and that. It was light gray in color with veins wrapped around it for extreme texture. "Sales are up for the entire demon collection. Interestingly enough, humans make up the largest percentage of those sales. Do you know why that is?"

"I don't know—*oh!*" Callum pushed at least half the incubus toy inside me, knocking a whimper from my lips.

"Don't you?" His cadence dropped to a rough whisper that scoured my flesh, making goosebumps explode over my skin. "Doesn't it look familiar?"

My breath hitched. It *did* look familiar. "It's modeled after your own dick."

His grin turned demonic, and he pushed the dildo inside me another inch, as if to confirm my suspicion. It was all the way inside me now, the spiked balls nudging my folds and making my nerves split apart with the fresh sensation.

Holy shit. What was he going to say when I told him I *owned* this one?

I wasn't sure what had driven me to buy the toy exactly. I'd first excused it as curiosity, but looking back, the idea of getting fucked by a fat demon dick had really turned me on. Which was weird, because I hadn't even known Callum was part demon. I'd only been aware of his angelic heritage.

"Callum... I have this one. I, I bought it..."

He fell still. "What?"

"When this came out, I bought it. It's the only Cupid-brand sex toy I've ever bought."

If I hadn't been completely convinced before, I was now. This connection I felt with Callum didn't have anything to do with Cupid's Arrow. This was fate. It had to be. It's why I'd felt a connection to him from day one. It's why I'd gone out and bought the one toy, out of the hundreds of toys the company sold, that was modeled after him.

"Callum. Don't you think that's a little too freaky to be coincidence? Maybe it was fate."

He pushed his face into mine, his lips peeling back to reveal serrated teeth. "There's no such thing as fate!" he hissed.

"T-then why would I buy a toy modeled after your dick?"

A barbed silence stretched over the room. Callum's ministrations ceased, leaving me impaled on the dildo.

Thoughts churned behind his stony gaze. I believed that we were fated, but it was a harder sell for this man who thought fated love could only be manufactured.

"Turns out that you never had to worry about breaking me with your true form. All this time, I've been training myself for you without even knowing it."

"It's not just my cock," he snapped. "I didn't think you'd want me with my wings. The eyes. The horns. Plus, my dick has a feature the toy doesn't."

Curiosity went off inside me with all the intensity of an

action-movie explosion. But there was another question burning in my throat that I had to ask first.

"I know you say there's no such thing as fate. Especially between a human and a supernatural. But maybe you're wrong. Maybe the potion isn't working on me—and I don't think it is—because we were already fated to be together. Why else would I have been drawn to buy that toy when I've never bought another sex toy in my entire life? Why would we feel such a pull toward one another?"

"That's not enough evidence," the dark angel seethed in a tone that warned me he was close to losing his temper.

"Oh yeah? Then how about this? If I were any other human, you wouldn't have cared at all that I betrayed you! You would have killed me and had the job posting listed on the internet the next fucking day." I picked up the chain, giving it a mocking rattle. "Look at this shit. This is next-level crazy! You're Callum Reaver. Nothing phases you... until now. You fucking lost it when you found out I betrayed Cupid Inc."

Something I'd said made the dark angel snap. He pulled the toy out, tossed it aside and his huge hands grasped my hips, yanking me off the counter. He spun me around so I was facing the mirror, and he pulled my rear against him, sliding his erection between my ass cheeks.

"Oh, sweet little bird. Make no fucking mistake. I *am* this company. I *am* Cupid. And I'll make you bleed for what you've done."

12

ROBIN

He slammed into my body with little warning, encasing himself fully inside my heat.

I released a ragged scream, my hands flying backward—to push him away or to pull him closer, I wasn't really sure. It was too much and somehow not enough.

I'd played with the toy modeled after his cock, but it wasn't *anything* like the real thing. He felt so much bigger and heavier inside me. The bumps, ridges and plump veins wrapping his shaft were more pronounced and hit parts of me the toy hadn't.

My eyes dropped to the sink, but his hand fisted my hair, forcing my gaze to the mirror. "Look!"

I found myself the main focus of countless beady, blood-red eyes, and two ocean-blue ones. They were as violent as a sea storm, and suddenly I felt myself drowning within them.

"You're going to fucking watch me ruin you!"

My cheeks flushed with a blush that streaked down to my chest, making my nipples rosy and red with need. My tits bounced with every savage thrust of his hips. Beads of sweat streaked down our flesh as everything shook—our breath, our bodies, our hearts, our entire world.

He thrust into me with punishing strokes that had my legs trembling violently within seconds. Every time he slammed into me, the marble countertop knocked painfully against my hips. The mass of him stretched me, his bumps and ridges scraping my insides.

This was primal.

This was painful.

And, fuck me, it was absolute perfection.

"That's it, pet. Take my cock." He smacked my ass hard, then chased it with another thrust. The tiny room was filled with the sounds of slapping flesh on flesh and the clatter of the chain.

The mirror steamed over as the room turned swampish with humidity. Callum pressed a wet kiss to my neck, just beneath my ear. "Remember what I said I was going to do to you?" he huffed out.

My mind scrambled for the answer. "M-make me bleed?"

"Mmm, that's the one." His hand roved over my chest, palming my breasts and tweaking my nipples until I moaned. "I'm going to do something to you. Something *deplorable*, Robin."

My heart skipped a beat.

What did he mean? Could it have something to do with his cock's *feature*, the one he'd left out of the toy version?

Everything in me went cold, then hot again. This was so wrong, yet it felt so right. How was that possible? I was chained up, for crying out loud. He'd put me in a cage. Now here he was, buried balls deep inside me while claiming me as his mate. How much more deplorable could it get?

He ceased the assault of his hips, but he didn't withdraw from me. We just stood there, suspended in time and space, his heaving breaths fanning down my spine.

"A-are you giving me an out? Because I don't recall you giving me a choice earlier."

I was in a pretty precarious position to run my mouth now, considering I was still impaled on him. But he only gave me a sinful smile. "You saw me spiking the drink. Yet, you took it anyway. So don't pretend I forced you."

My throat constricted. I should have known. Of course he knew that I'd seen him. He had eyes everywhere, literally. He also probably heard my reaction, from my breathing to my heart rate. He also probably picked up on the subtle shift in my scent when I'd realized I was finally going to be with Callum.

"If you saw me, then you know I took it because I want to be with you. The Callum I've known for three years, and the monster I'm just starting to know. I want to see the worst parts of you, Callum."

"Because you think you deserve punishment?"

"Because I think I deserve you, both the good and the bad."

"The bad," he echoed on a dark chuckle that filled the entire room and reverberated through my skull. "You're right about that. You do deserve the bad after what you've done. But that won't stop me from making you mine."

He resumed his thrusts, his rhythm more relaxed. Each punch of his pelvis was devastating, though, the claiming pressure in my pussy growing heavier. Unrelenting. Earth shattering.

He was so huge I swear I could almost feel him in my throat.

With one hand, he took the chain hanging from my neck and lifted it, slipping his other beneath it. He scraped my skin lightly with his needle-sharp talon, then he changed the angle of his finger and *pushed.*

I didn't scream, didn't pull away. I just stood there, taking his cock from behind and his claw gouging into my chest.

Callum was literally carving something into my chest, but I couldn't see what it was. I didn't dare look down, and the mirror was too fogged over to see shit.

The juxtaposition was debilitating—the pleasure of his cock pushing me toward complete paradise and the agony of his talon knifing my chest.

I couldn't think straight; I could hardly stand. All I could do was just stand there and *take it*.

Take his brutality.

Take his twisted love.

And I would. I'd take everything he had to give me. I would give up everything else in my life for him. When this was all over and we'd gotten all this pent-up lust and resentment out of our systems, I wondered if he'd do the same for me.

There was his father's company, which was his entire life. Then there was me. Something told me there wasn't going to be enough room in his dark heart for both of us.

My blood dripped into his porcelain sink, and I watched the bright streaks of my life force dribble down the drain.

So much blood.

What was he writing into my skin, a whole fucking novel? It felt like he was taking forever, but then again, I think he was purposely taking his time. When I was close to my breaking point, his hand dropped away from his canvas and his bloody hand gripped my hair, tugging my head back to force my gaze to the mirror.

"Wipe it."

It took my hazy brain a beat to process what he meant. With a trembling hand, I reached up to wipe the fog from the mirror.

The sight before me was utterly shocking. Sinful. Unholy depravity.

I was bent over, naked, with a metal collar clamped around my throat and the thick, metal chain clanking against the marble counter every time the terrifying male behind me pounded into me.

His wings were fully stretched out, countless eyes burning into me. Blood oozed from the two words he'd carved into my chest.

BE MINE.

His one hand that was stained with blood fisted my hair, and his other clasped around my throat above my collar, cutting off my air.

This was so intensely fucked up. He was torment incarnate. He was as brutal as I'd imagined, as he'd warned me he'd be.

I understood now why he'd always kept me at a safe distance.

Callum Reaver was half angel, half demon. He was Heaven and Hell.

Pleasure and pain.

Salvation and suffering.

But his cruel and callous nature evolved into this dark, sensual and wickedly intimate thing.

"Will you be mine, sweet little bird?" he asked in a featherlight whisper against my ear.

It was with his words of silk, the reflection of his body bowed possessively over mine, sweaty, bloody, bodies tangled together in an intimate kiss, that had me coming with a scream.

Every nerve ending in my body lit up and glorious bliss washed through me, making all the pain ebb away as I was taken to the absolute crux of paradise by my demon. But there he was, savagely jerking me back as he squeezed my throat tighter, making my vision spotty and my veins flare with hellfire.

"Answer me!"

"Yes!" I screamed. "I'll be yours, Callum!"

"That's a good girl." When he pulled out, I whirled around—too fast. My knees gave out, but he was there, swooping me up into his strong embrace. "You did such a good job for me," he praised.

There was that tender side to him, like salve over the pain he'd caused. "Aren't you going to finish?"

"Oh, little one. I'm only getting started. From now on, I'm going to live between your thighs."

He carried me to the shower and scrubbed me clean.

We stood there in silence, my gaze glued to the drain as I watched the cum- and blood-laced water swirl down.

Something had shifted between the two of us now that he'd claimed me.

Something that had nothing to do with Cupid's Arrow.

13

CALLUM

Something was happening to me. As I'd fucked my secretary's gorgeous cunt and felt her walls twitch and shudder around me, it was like finding a missing puzzle piece—or more accurately, a lock snapping into place. Like an invisible collar around my neck to match Robin's.

This didn't feel like retribution for her betrayal, nor did it feel like a punishment.

This felt like freedom, even though I knew from this day forward I'd be a slave to Robin's body, her soul and her heart.

I took my time cleaning her in the shower, making this last. I never wanted this to end. She was like the breath of air I knew I needed, but never let myself have.

Now that she was here, and mine, I didn't know breathing her in would be this cathartic.

This whole infernal building, this entire existence of living in my father's shadow, was suffocating. With her, a weight was lifted off my chest.

I couldn't keep my talons off of her. I hadn't touched her, or any woman for that matter, for three years. It was like I was a wild bear coming out of hibernation, and I was ravenous for every drop I could possibly milk from her. Her tears, her blood, her piss, her cum.

I needed more of her, so much so that I could barely think straight.

I'd held myself back from coming inside her. She might have played with the incubus toy modeled after my own dick, but it lacked a very specific feature that I wanted her to be lying down for.

It seemed silly washing the blood and cum off her; I was only going to cover her in more. But I needed a moment to calm down and collect my shattered senses.

She was like a potent drug. I was high on her, and if I wasn't careful, I'd rip her open and gorge myself on her until there was nothing left.

That's exactly what I'd been afraid of. It was why I hadn't let myself cross too far over the line with her.

After several minutes of excruciating silence, she turned around and gasped when she found I'd shifted back to my human form. I'd only done it because it had been cramped with my wings inside the glass enclosure. Plus, I'd needed a moment to center myself.

Her lower lip trembled, and she stepped closer to me, her head coming to rest against my chest. Her fingers trailed over my heart-and-arrow tattoo.

"I missed you..."

"I'm still me, Robin. I'm the same man, no matter what form I choose to present."

She took a step back, meeting my gaze easily when there was only one set of eyes to focus on. "You're more vicious in your other form."

Her hand pulled away from my chest to point at hers. The bloody wound reading "BE MINE" still wept tears of red down her pretty little tits. It hadn't been that deep of a cut.

Thank fuck for that. If it had, I wouldn't forgive myself. "I don't think you would have done this to me if you hadn't shifted. If you'd kept your human form—"

"I'm *not* human. Remember that, Robin."

Her line of sight dropped to our feet, her expression indecipherable.

I caressed her chin in my palm, tilting her head so her eyes locked with mine. "You told me something that stuck with me. You said you didn't feed the supernatural hate group internal intel because you're a xenophobe, but because you wanted to shut down the Cupid's Arrow project. Tell me again, and this time I'm going to try harder to believe you."

Slowly, this female was melting the ice around my heart. I wanted to trust her, desperately. Plus, it was hard to ignore the stacking evidence that maybe we were naturally fated mates. Something had compelled her to buy one Cupid-brand sex toy among a sea of options, and the fact that I had been the model for that toy had been kept under wraps. Plus, she'd seen me spike her drink with the love potion and she'd taken it anyway, proving that she really did want me. Then, there was that magnetism we'd had since day one.

Even with all that, I still needed to hear her say it.

"I meant it, Callum." Tears fell from her cheeks, and her eyelashes fluttered as the salty water rolled down her chest and into her wound. "I don't hate supernaturals. How could I? I've been in love with one for three years."

Time stood still.

Had she said what I thought she'd said?

She loved me. My breathing accelerated. My heart—the one I'd thought had shriveled and blackened by now—sang with joy.

I didn't think she could love a monster like me, not after seeing what I truly was. Not after learning on a very personal level just how fucked up I could be, especially in my true form.

Could it be true that her heart and soul beat for me, all on their own? That she betrayed me because that was Robin? She was going to do what she thought was right, and the trial testing for Cupid's Arrow had been cruel. My attention centered on the collar around her neck, then lowered to the bloody letters etched into her flesh.

I had always been one for extremes, and it looks like I wasn't alone.

What a pair we made.

"I can prove it," she said, reaching back to turn off the water. Taking me by the hand, she led me out of the suite and back into my office.

She stood directly in front of the floor-to-ceiling windows, completely bare. We were high up in the building, but not so high that the people on the street wouldn't be able to see her if anyone happened to look up. Night was beginning to fall, so the light from my office would illuminate anything, especially in front of the window.

"Take my collar off, Callum."

My eyes narrowed. She wasn't asking me, she was demanding it. But the collar and chain had just been a symbol when all this started, a physical reminder that she was mine. She didn't need it anymore. She had my marks on her chest. And pretty soon, she'd have my cock stuffed inside her. Those were the only things she needed to be reminded that she belonged to me.

I strode to my desk and opened one of the drawers, retrieving the key to the padlock securing the collar.

"Hold your hair up, and turn around."

She slowly turned so that she was facing the window with her back to me. Her hands swept under her long, chestnut hair and pulled it off her neck. A second later, I had the lock off, and the metal clattered to the floor at our feet.

She flipped back around, rubbing the impression the collar had left. "Thanks. I kind of liked it, actually."

I smirked at my little masochist, loving her more with each passing moment. "You are a strange female, little bird. Maybe you really are fated to be mine." My smile darkened. "What a sad and twisted fate for you."

She chewed her bottom lip. "Twisted, yes. But sad? No. What's sad is the people down there..." She glanced out the window, gesturing at the protesters on the street corner with their signs.

God said marriage is between man and woman. Not man and beast, one of the signs read.

Tch. They were the real animals.

"I used these people to get the word out about Cupid's Arrow and stir up a media nightmare so you'd shut it down. I want to prove once and for all that I'm not really one of them."

"How?"

"I want you to take me, right here, where they can see."

14

CALLUM

Robin wanted me to fuck her against the window, in front of all the anti-supernatural protesters. I hadn't taken her for an exhibitionist. Then again, there were a lot of things I'd discovered about my new mate today.

She wanted them to watch me take her.

Such a naughty request, one that had me prowling toward her with a visceral hunger stirring between my legs. All it took was the mental image of her naked body pressed up against the glass for everyone to see, and I was shifting.

Her eyes widened, her head craning back to maintain eye contact with me as my height grew by two heads at least. With my four wings extended and my celestial sight engaged, I saw all of her. The beating of her heart, the blood surging through her veins. The way her inner walls were clenching in antici-pation for me.

I almost wished she were still clothed, just so I could shred them off her right before fucking her against the window.

I'd start gently this time. I hadn't done that yet, and she

needed to see that I was capable of being civilized when the occasion called for it.

I ran the tips of my talons over her plush lips and she stuck her tongue out, swirling it around my finger before nipping the tip.

I tugged her closer to me with a playful growl, palming her tits in my hands. She was so small in my grip. I was also learning that she wasn't as fragile as she appeared.

She received my brutal kisses like they were sweet pecks, wore my collar like it was a dainty necklace and took my rough fucking like it was sweet love making.

She really was made for me.

I was already convinced. This wasn't an angle she was trying to play for survival or the potion at work. I knew she felt that invisible tether, pulling us closer and closer until we could barely tell ourselves apart.

She didn't have to prove anything anymore. I believed everything that passed through those sweet lips.

But that didn't mean I was about to turn down her offer of showing her off.

I wasn't exactly an exhibitionist, but who the hell was I to deny a chance to fuck my human mate in front of a group of people who hated nothing more than couplings between supernaturals and humans?

I grabbed her by the shoulders and spun her around, pushing her belly-first against the window.

She whimpered when her tits collided with the cool glass.

"Spread those ass cheeks, little bird. Show me what belongs to me."

Her hands came around to grip the rounded globes of her ass, and she pulled them apart to expose her cunt to me. She was already soaking wet, her arousal making her inner thighs glisten.

I pushed into her slowly, reveling in the way she quivered around me. The heat of her pussy gripped me like a perfectly tailored glove.

Like she'd been made for me by some greater force.

Her moans made her entire body vibrate, and I stroked in and out. Fuck. She was so hot and slick for me, allowing me to burrow in deep.

"Callum, they've noticed us!"

I thought I'd care. Now that I was inside her, I didn't.

That's when it hit me.

In a single day, I'd changed. Dramatically. All I cared about was her.

She was mine to fuck.

Mine to love.

Mine to keep.

Mine.

I withdrew from her and spun her around before slamming her back into the glass. I was inside her again on the next breath, her legs banding around my waist. I used the leverage of the window to drive into her as deep as I could, the force rattling the glass dangerously.

I kissed her with all the pent-up frustration, resentment and bitter feelings from the betrayal. And as our lips clashed together, it all evaporated.

Like magic.

Like fate.

Looping one arm beneath her, I carried her to my desk. With one swipe, everything on top of it, including my computer, crashed to the floor. I laid her down on the smooth surface, positioning her legs so they dangled over the side. Bracing my hands on either side of her head, I resumed my strokes.

I didn't know what it was about this woman that made me

so feral, so mindless with hunger. Maybe it was the way she peered up at me through those thick lashes, or how she ground her hips to impale herself further onto me. But my gods, I couldn't hold back any longer.

I fucked her, my tempo climbing, knot and all.

"Fuck, Callum. I, I don't know how much more I can take," she cried.

"You'll take everything I give you," I lashed out through a malevolent grin that curled the corners of my mouth.

She arched her hips off the desk as much as my weight would allow, begging for more of me. Then her hands flew to my horns, holding on to them for dear life as I railed her atop my desk. Her fingers curled around them, mimicking the motion my cock was making but on a smaller scale. And it was then that I roared my release, spurting my seed deep within her.

She moaned, her head rolling to the side. I grasped her chin and forced her to look at me.

"Do you feel that, little bird?" I panted through shuddering breaths. "This is what you do to me. You crawl beneath my skin, invade my senses and you fucking *obliterate* me."

She screamed, her pussy clamping around me again.

Her eyelashes fluttered, and her tits heaved as she mewled my name. Christ. She was so pretty when she came for me. Imagining her heavy with my child triggered something primal within me.

She tensed up when she felt it. The center of my shaft had swelled, creating a knot that locked me inside her. "W-what's that?"

I watched her intently, slowing down. "You've worked for this company long enough. You've seen the few toys we have with this particular feature. You tell me what it is."

She blinked up at me, and I could see the gears turning.

Then her entire body flushed with a delicious blush as realization hit her. "It's a knot. You have a knot! I thought only werewolves had those."

"It's fairly common for incubi as well."

She sucked in a gasp and squirmed on my dick as the center continued to swell. "It... it feels good. I feel—" She paused, searching for the words. "Like a little bird. Trapped. Like I can't move."

I arched a brow. "In a good way?"

Her pussy pulsated, and I had my answer before the words left her. "In the best way."

15

ROBIN

We laid like that until the sky went dark and the day bled into the next. The swelling of the knot had gone down and, to my dismay, he pulled out.

My toy certainly hadn't been able to do that.

Even after he'd pulled out, he held me tightly, tracing the lettering he'd carved into my flesh.

"It doesn't bother you that I'm a sadist?" he asked after a little while. "Chains and bloodplay may be a semi-frequent occurrence. They weren't just because I was mad at you. I really enjoy those things."

I chewed my bottom lip—something I always did when I was immersed in thought. "I like them too. There's only one thing that bothers me about you, Callum, and it has nothing to do with your kinks."

He propped himself up on his elbow, his brows bending into a scowl. "Ah, yes. My devotion to my father's evil corporation, and the lack of morals required to be its CEO. Trust me, I hate that too."

"If you hate it so much, why are you here?"

"What else do I have?"

I sat up, tugging lightly at his horn. A purring growl grumbled from his chest. "You have me, Callum. You know, people do say it's possible for human-supernatural couples to feel that 'fated' pull toward one another."

He heaved a sigh. "I don't like calling it fate."

I frowned at him, discerning the pain in his words. "Why?"

He shrugged one shoulder. "People say it's the work of the gods. And if they are gods, why did they forsake me and have my mother abandon me at a young age? Why did they give me an abusive father who solely loved his work, just for him to die and leave his only son and his precious corporation behind?"

"Oh, Callum..."

He ducked his head, kissing my shoulder. "None of that, now. I've healed from it, I think."

Warmth wound through my chest. "Really?"

"Mmm. Maybe sending me you was the gods' way of making up for the cards they dealt. So I suppose I can believe in fate after all."

It was hard to find the words to describe my happiness, but I kept my face serious as I debated asking the question burning on the tip of my tongue. It was personal, but then again, what between us wasn't anymore?

"Why did your mother leave?"

His gaze snapped to mine, and for a second I thought he might not answer my question. But I felt his muscles unwind as he relaxed into me. "My mother may have been a demon, but she was kindhearted, like you. She hated this company, so one day she forced my father to choose: Her or being Cupid. He chose Cupid. She tried to take me away with her, but he wouldn't let her. They fought and fought, then it turned physically violent."

The angel went quiet for a few beats. "He killed her. I... I don't think he meant to."

"Oh my god, Callum. I'm so sorry," I muttered as horror wound through me, not really knowing what else to say.

"Thank you, but it was a long time ago. My father carried the guilt and shame of it around for years. Eventually, I think it's what killed him."

"That's awful."

"It scares me how much of him I see in myself as the years go by. Similarities."

There was another long span of silence. "I'm not going to be like him, Robin. I'm not going to choose my company over the people I love."

I stared at him. "What are you going to do?"

He fell quiet, contemplating his answer. It felt like an eternity passed. Then suddenly, he was on his feet, rushing around his office like a madman. Something had shifted within him. Something was different, not just with him, but with both of us.

I sat up, watching him hurry around with inhuman speed. "What are you doing?"

"You asked what I'm going to do. I'm going to burn it down."

I waited for the punchline. The crack in his serious mien. The laugh. A twitch of his lips. Something that would indicate that he was joking.

"What?"

He stepped into his pants and threw me a change of clothes. "I'm going to burn this place down to the fucking ground, Robin. I refuse to follow in my father's footsteps one second longer."

I took another moment to search for any trace of a jest. Nothing. "Oh my god. You're serious."

"Deadly."

He shifted back to his human form, continuing to rush around. A zippo lighter was suddenly in his hands. "I'm going to burn it down, pin it on the xenophobes—it will be easy—and collect some insurance money for extra pocket change. Then we'll start fresh. We'll still manufacture the toys, but the chemical plants, the love formulas, it's over. I should have shut it down a long time ago."

He stopped and turned toward me, a look on his face that made all the anxiety clawing at my chest crumble to ash.

I'd been right. I suspected there'd be a time when Callum would have to choose between me and his dad's company.

And he was choosing me.

I hopped down from the desk, brandishing a wicked smirk. "I'll get the fire alarm."

I stood on the corner of the block, gaping up at the building I'd worked in for the past three years as it went up in flames. A crowd had started to form, police lights flashed and firemen worked frantically to put out the fire.

It was too late to save it. Callum had ensured that.

The xenophobe protesters were chanting "this is God's judgment." It put a bitter taste in my mouth, but my dark angel didn't seem the least bit phased. He just tucked me close against him, a deliciously dark smile tugging at his lips as he ducked his head down and whispered, "In the end, they made a smart move recruiting you. They got what they wanted. Well, maybe not exactly what they wanted. Supernatural kind isn't just going to burst into flames, but to them, this is probably the next best thing."

"You really don't have any regrets?"

He took my chin, cradling it tenderly in his hand while he brought our lips together in a dark and decadent kiss. "No, Robin. Just like with those doves three years ago, you set me free from that fucking cage."

"You aren't even a little sad that your home is gone?"

"I have a new home," he assured me, his hand coming up to curve around the back of my neck. "And she's right here in front of me."

I was so happy, I could cry. It was weird to say that, considering that almost everything I'd known for the last three years was literally going up in flames.

But I had what was important right here. "Happy Valentine's Day, Callum."

"Happy Valentine's Day, little bird."

The End

Authors Note

Thank you for reading Bleed for Cupid! If you enjoyed Callum and Robin's story, please consider leaving a review!

If you're wanting more dark and spicy little monster romance bites in the Holiday Horrors series, make sure you're following me at any of these links to hear about future additions to the series <3